Lake of the Big Snake

An African Rain Forest Adventure

by Isaac Olaleye

Illustrated by Claudia Shepard

Boyds Mills Press

Published by Caroline House
Boyds Mills Press, Inc.
A Highlights Company
815 Church Street
Honesdale, Pennsylvania 18431
Printed in China

Publisher Cataloging-in-Publication Data
Olaleye, Isaac
Lake of the big snake / by Isaac Olaleye ; illustrated by
Claudia Shepard.—1st.ed.
[32] p. : col.ill. ; cm.
Summary: Two boys outwit a hungry snake in an African rain forest village.
ISBN 1-56397-096-1
1. Africa—Juvenile fiction. 2. Snakes—Fiction—Juvenile literature.
[1. Africa—Fiction. 2. Snakes—Fiction.] I. Shepard, Claudia, ill.
II. Title.
[E]—dc21   1998   CIP
Library of Congress Catalog Card Number 95-80780

First edition, 1998
Book designed by Tim Gillner
The text of this book is set in 15-point Hiroshige Book.
The illustrations are done in watercolors.

10 9 8 7 6 5 4 3 2

To Judy Ross Enderle—my editor and cherished friend
—I. O.

To Xavier and Adrian Baldwin and family, the children of Detroit,
and my new grandson, Austin Robert Shepard
—C. S.

AUTHOR'S NOTE

Near my village in Nigeria, among a rich confusion of green, is a large swampy lake. I have many pleasant memories of that lake. I remember lying in my hut on quiet nights listening to a chorus of frogs singing across the water. During the dry seasons, I remember watching a blizzard of butterflies rise up from the water's edge. But the lake was home to more than just frogs and butterflies. People believed that a monstrous snake, perhaps an anaconda, lived in its muddy brown waters. That's why they called the lake Ode Ere— "Lake of the Big Snake."

This story is based on my childhood memories. The villages of Iloko and Inisa are real places. They are near Èrín, the village where I grew up. There are words in this story that may be unfamiliar, unless you've been to Nigeria. A *danziki* is a brightly-colored shirt with short, wide sleeves. A cassava is like a potato, but it is bigger and longer. A panpala tree is called different names in various parts of my country. This tree is not commonly found in the part of the rain forest where I grew up. But I remember seeing a few of them, and the memory of those trees has stayed with me.

When I was a child, I liked to hear stories about Odo Ere and the big snake that lived there. Now I've written one myself. I hope you enjoy it!

—Isaac

In an African rain forest village called Inisa, lived two boys, Ade and Tayo. Best friends they were.

And best friends
their mothers were.

One day Ade's mother said, "Tayo's mother and I are going to Iloko Village. While we're gone, sweep the hut, inside and out."

Tayo's mother said to her son, "Peel all the
cassavas. We will have them for dinner."
"Do not leave the village,"
the mothers warned their sons.

Then with bundles on their heads,
the two women disappeared
into the jungle.

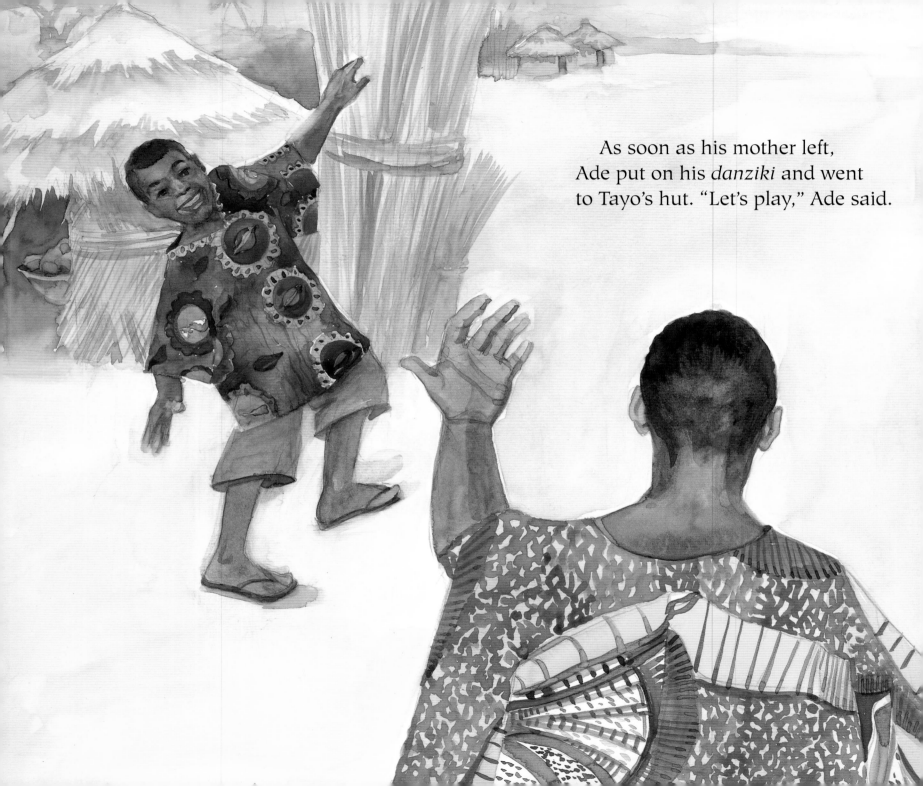

As soon as his mother left,
Ade put on his *danziki* and went
to Tayo's hut. "Let's play," Ade said.

"No! My mother will be angry if all the cassavas are not peeled," Tayo said.

"Only for a few minutes," Ade said. "Please!" he begged.

"Well . . . all right," said Tayo. So Tayo left the cassavas and put on his only *danziki*.

Gidi-gidi, *gidi-gidi*, the boys galloped toward the edge of the village.

A sloping trail they followed, and into the dark, deep jungle they disappeared.

Across a babbling brook lay an open field. And at the edge of the field, where towering trees stood, was a lake.

Gidi-gidi, gidi-gidi, the boys galloped toward
the lake as if by a magnet they were pulled.

The lake was called Odo Ere,
or Lake of the Big Snake.

Plants on the other side of the lake
were heavy with sweet berries. Mmmm!

"Let's go get some," Ade said.

"No!" blurted Tayo. "Maybe we should
go home now."

Ade began wading *sosh-sash, sosh-sash*
across the narrow and shallow part of the lake.

Popping a few berries into his mouth,
Ade exclaimed, "They taste like sugarcane!"
Sosh-sash. Sosh-sash. Tayo crossed too.
Delicious berries exploded in their mouths.
Mmmm!
Their pockets bulged with more berries.

Sssoshsh! A sudden splash sent ripples across
the still lake.

"A snake . . . a big water snake," Ade said
in a trembling voice.

Toward the narrow part of the lake
the boys scrambled.

Sosh-sash, sosh-sash, they tried to cross.

But toward them the snake slithered smoothly!

Hurry! *Sosh-sash, sosh-sash,*
the boys splashed back to the shore,
where they scrambled back and forth, back and forth.
But the snake lay in the way—waiting, watching!

The narrow part of the lake was too wide to jump.

And the rest of the lake was too deep to wade.

The boys were trapped!

"I told you. Didn't I say we shouldn't cross?
Ade, it's all your fault!," cried Tayo.

"No, it's not," argued Ade. "You crossed on your own!"

"But you said, 'Mmmm! The berries taste like sugarcane!'"

"That didn't mean you had to cross," Ade said.

The boys blamed each other back and forth, back and forth
But as shadows grew longer, they stopped bickering
and began to figure out a way to outsmart the hungry monster.
"The snake will swim away if it can't see us,"
Tayo said.
The boys hid behind a panpala tree.
The snake flickered its tongue.
Feeling the heat from the boys' bodies,
the snake knew exactly where they hid!
And the snake did not swim away.

"Let's climb," Ade said.

So they climbed to the tree's
V-shaped trunk. The trunk hardly had enough
room for two feet.

The snake flickered its tongue again.
It still knew exactly where the boys were!

Ade grabbed a limb, held it with his
left hand, and whacked it with his right foot.

Taa paa, the limb broke in half.

He hurled one of the limbs at the snake.
It landed limply on the water and floated.
The snake rolled its eyes, but did not budge.

"We are going to be eaten up," Tayo moaned.
"Mother said not to leave the village," Ade said.
"We should have listened!" cried Tayo.
"Wait! I have another idea," Ade said.
"Another idea!" Tayo said. "You had this idea
   and look what happened."

"Just listen. Hide behind the tree,"
Ade told Tayo.

"I will tease the snake away from the
narrow part. And as the snake follows me,
dash across. Okay?"

Zzt, zzt, Ade teased the snake.
The snake eyed Ade greedily.
Gidi-gidi, gidi-gidi, Tayo ran.
He glanced left, and right.
The snake was not in sight!
Sosh-sash, sosh-sash, sash, sash, sash.
Tayo crossed. Whew!

It was now Ade's turn to cross.

On the other shore, Tayo got the snake's attention by making a splash. Tayo's feet pounded at the edge of the lake, *whack, whack, whack-lap, whack-lap*.

Suddenly, Tayo was sinking! Quicksand!

Quickly, he lay flat on his back, spread his arms, and held still. He stopped sinking.

"Get up! Get up!" shouted Ade, "Before the snake comes."

Nervously, Ade made a splash, clapped,
and stepped *thump-bump, thump-bump*
on his side of the lake. And the snake was distracted!
   Whew!
   Wiggle-wriggle-roll, Tayo grasped the frond
of a tender lady fern. But the frond broke!
   "Help! Help!" Tayo yelled.
But his voice wasn't strong enough
to be heard in the distant village.
   Thump-bump, thump-bump,
Ade marched on the other shore.

Wiggle-wriggle-roll, Tayo grabbed hold
of two of the fern's fronds.

Wiggle-wriggle-roll, Tayo almost
uprooted the fern before he uprooted himself
from the quicksand.

Wiggle-wriggle-roll. Tayo was safe at last on the firm ground.
But Ade was still stuck on the other shore.
And the snake had not gone away.

Tayo took off his only *danziki*.
Small rocks he put inside the *danziki*.
And at a wide edge of the lake he laid the *danziki*.
   Now Tayo clapped and made noises, *"Te-te, te-te, te-te,"*
teasing the snake to where the *danziki* was.
Into the lake he tossed the *danziki*.
And the snake caught the scent of Tayo in the *danziki!*
And the snake slithered toward the *danziki!*
   Ade ran *gidi-gidi, gidi-gidi,* to the narrow
and shallow part of the lake.

The snake was not in sight!
Sosh-sash, sosh-sash, sash, sash, sash, sash.
Ade dashed to safety!

Whew! Hurrah! Hurrah! Hurrah!

Ade and Tayo locked in a joyful embrace.

"My mother is going to be very mad at me for losing my only *danziki*," Tayo said as he cleaned up at the brook.

"Don't worry," Ade said. "I have two *danzikis*. I'll give you one. And I will stand by you when your mother punishes you."

Then arm in arm, running a little, *gidi-gidi, gidi-gidi,* and walking a little, *pek-pek, pek-pek,* Ade and Tayo scurried toward the village to face their mothers together.